CW00853237

OTHER BOOKS

IT'S A KID'S LIFE
NEW
NEW
NEW
NEW
NEW
NEW
NEW
KERRY GIBB
ILLUSTRATED BY ELLIE BARRETT

IT'S A KID'S LIFE
Arch-Enemies
KERRY GIBB
ILLUSTRATED BY ELLIE BARRETT

IT'S A KID'S LIFE
double digits
KERRY GIBB
ILLUSTRATED BY ELLIE BARRETT

Subscribe now to

Author Kerry Gibb

on YouTube for some

behind the scenes videos, book

reviews, top 10 count downs,

chances to win some great prizes,

and much more!

Also follow Kerry Gibb on Facebook,

Instagram, and Twitter!

To Raffy

IT'S A KID'S LIFE

4

CHRISTMAS COUNTDOWN

By Kerry Gibb

Published by Packman Publishing.

First edition published in Great Britain 2018 .

Printed and bound in Great Britain at Clays Ltd, Elcograf S.p.A.

A CIP catalogue record for this title is available from the British Library.

ISBN 978-0-9934937-3-7

For Liam, Jamie, Danny, and Joe, and every child who loves Christmas!

This is me, Ben,
age 10.

Pocket Rocket, my 8
year old brother.

Big Spud, my 5
year old brother.

Little Spud, my 3
year old brother.

Dad - real dad to my brothers, and technically step-dad to me, but basically, the best dad I could ask for.

Mum - makes great hot chocolate and marshmallows, but can be embarrassing!

Rob - technically my real dad, but never been too good at the dad stuff.

Cassie - Rob's girlfriend and Jodie's Mum.

Jodie - my baby sister.

CHAPTER 1

It was December the 1st. The most exciting month of the year was upon us. The month where you get to eat chocolate from your advent calendar every morning before breakfast. The month where everyone forgets about the cost of electricity as they cover the front of their houses with dazzling lights. The month where instead of being told 'No,' when you ask your parents for something, they tell you to 'write it on your Christmas list.' The month where everyone seems to be that little bit happier and friendlier than usual.

And let's not forget, the very important issue of two whole weeks off school! The only downside of that was the six extra hours a day that I would have to endure my three younger brothers irritating me.

I have been known to describe my little brothers as being more annoying than an ant nibbling on my bottom cheek. And if you have ever had the misfortune of sitting on an ants' nest, you'll know exactly what I'm talking about!

I could hear all three of them right now in fact, next door in Pocket Rocket's bedroom. Feeling suspicious as to why my eight year old brother had allowed the highly irritating younger two into his bedroom, without trapping them in a headlock or a double nelson, I paused outside his door to listen.

"Dear Spuds... that means you two," I heard Pocket Rocket say to Big Spud and Little Spud. "I would love to put you on my nice list this year, but I'm afraid that you have been far too naughty lately."

I heard my two youngest brothers gasp in horror as he said this. I pressed my ear closer to the door as I eavesdropped on them.

"Don't worry though, boys," Pocket Rocket continued. "There is a way you can avoid getting a big, fat lump of coal in your stocking this Christmas Eve. You can guarantee a nice lot of presents instead by doing the following things...

1. Tell Mum that it was in fact you who ate half of the box of chocolates that Mum bought for her friend, and not Pocket Rocket."

Now it was my turn to gasp in horror. It just wasn't true! I had seen Pocket Rocket shove half of the box into his greedy mouth last week before resealing it. Poor Mum had looked mortified when her friend had opened her present to find a half empty box of chocolates.

I was about to burst into my brother's room to demand to know what was going on when I heard Pocket Rocket announcing number two on the list.

"2. Do both of your big brothers' chores for the whole of December."

Hmm, I quite like the sound of that, I thought to myself.

"3. You must stop watching babyish cartoons, and instead, put on anything your brothers want to see."

This was sounding better by the second.

"4. Tell your mum and dad that Pocket Rocket deserves to have the biggest present of all of you this Christmas, as he is their favourite son."

Suddenly things weren't sounding quite so appealing. I pulled on the door handle, and burst into Pocket Rocket's bedroom. He was sitting on his bed with a piece of paper in his hand. Big Spud and Little Spud were sitting silently on his rug, like obedient little school children listening to their teacher. They were gazing up at him with their big, innocent, blue eyes, taking in every word that he was saying. Pocket Rocket jumped when he saw me, and hid the piece of paper behind his back whilst whispering, "Lots of love Father Christmas," to our little brothers.

The sneaky little thing! He had written a pretend letter from Father Christmas to trick our younger brothers into doing things for his benefit. I was about to spoil his cunning plan by telling Big Spud and Little Spud that it was actually Pocket Rocket who had written the letter and not Father Christmas, when I remembered the bit about doing 'both of your big brother's chores'. Maybe I should play along with Pocket Rocket after all. As much fun as it would be to expose him for the devious big brother he was, it would be even funnier to see my two younger brothers suffer.

I imagined them struggling up the stairs with the vacuum cleaner. I had always thought how unfair it was that I was repeatedly given this chore as they were 'too little' to carry it, according to Mum. It was about time those two started to pull their weight. Pocket Rocket looked at me, his eyes silently begging me to play along.

"Wow, that's so exciting," I said in a big animated voice. "A real letter from Father Christmas! You two are so lucky. You had better make sure you do what he says, though. It would be horrible if you woke up to a lump of coal on Christmas morning rather than a stocking overflowing with presents."

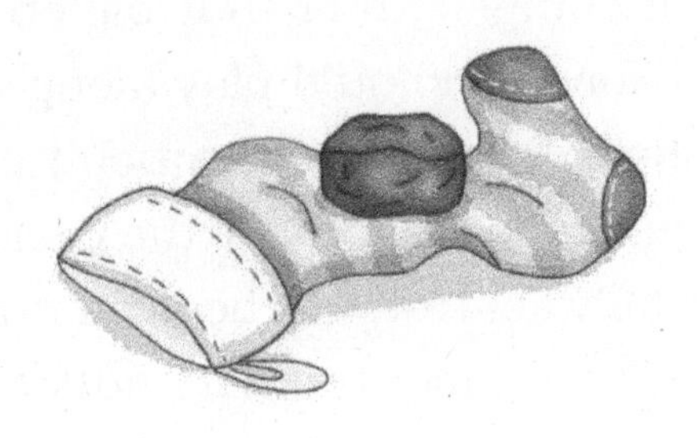

My two brothers looked at me like I had just told them they were going to have to eat cold porridge (with no syrup!) for the rest of their lives.

They then turned to stare at each other before running out of the room shouting for Mum, presumably to take the blame for the chocolate incident.

Pocket Rocket and I grinned at each other like the cats who'd got the cream.

"Let me see that," I said, swiping the letter from 'Father Christmas' from behind his back. The lazy thing hadn't even bothered to write it properly. He had just put a load of squiggles instead, knowing that Big Spud and Little Spud couldn't read very well yet.

"I like your style," I said to my brother. "But, there's no way in the world that Mum and Dad will fall for your little plan to get the best present at Christmas. And if they are stupid enough to fall for it, I will make sure I tell them to do the exact opposite. Capiche?"

'Capiche' means 'understand' in Italian, and Dad was a big fan of saying this to us after giving us a lecture about something. I could see why he liked to say it now. It had a much better ring to it than 'understand'.

Pocket Rocket rolled his eyes and mumbled "OK", knowing that he had probably pushed his plan a bit too far with this request.

"Come on," I said. "Let's go and ask Mum if we can decorate the tree."

Pocket Rocket didn't need asking twice. He had always loved putting up the Christmas tree. All we had to do now was figure out a way to get Dad out of the house, so that we could actually enjoy doing it. Dad always spoiled it by shouting at us that we were doing it all wrong!

CHAPTER 2

"I don't see why I have to go right this second," grumbled Dad as Mum practically shoved him out of the front door.

"Because Obi and Lola told me they want their Daddy to walk them today," Mum replied.

Obi and Lola were sitting by the front door, wagging their tails in anticipation of the walk they were about to go on.

Dad started to protest that a) dogs can't talk, and b) he was NOT their 'daddy', when Mum reminded him how the pub down the road was very dog friendly. She suggested that he stop there for a pint of beer by the open fire on his way home from the walk. We all knew at that point that Mum's plan had worked. Mum knew Dad's weakness – a nice cold pint of beer!

She waved him goodbye as Dad quickly hurried off down the driveway, seizing his chance to escape before Mum could change her mind.

“Right boys,” she said, coming into the lounge. “Mission – get the Christmas tree up without Dad interfering, is underway!”

‘Last Christmas’ by Wham started coming out of Dad’s new speaker as Mum connected her laptop to it. It had taken a while, but she was finally coming round to the fact that this wasn’t 1999 anymore, and you didn’t need a CD player to listen to your favourite music. She said something about listening to cassette tapes when she was a little girl once, but she gave up trying to explain what they were when we all just looked at her with blank faces like she was from another planet.

"This song's rubbish," moaned Little Spud. "Put Justin Beaver on!"

"For the one hundredth time, Little Spud, it's not BEAVER!" moaned Big Spud.

"BEAVER, BEAVER, BEAVER!" shouted a disgruntled Little Spud.

"BIEBER, BIEBER, BIEBER!" retaliated Big Spud, even louder.

Their argument was suddenly drowned out as the soft tones of Last Christmas were replaced by Eminem belting out 'Lose Yourself'. Pocket Rocket had taken charge of the laptop.

"Sorry boys," said Mum as she nudged Pocket Rocket away from the controls. "It's tradition. Christmas songs only whilst we put up the Christmas tree. Right Ben?" she asked, looking at me for support.

I nodded, knowing that this was one thing that my brothers would not get their own way over. Mum loved Christmas as much as we did, and traditions like listening to Christmas songs as we put up the tree were important to her. Most of the songs were pretty awful, but there was something special about doing it every year that stopped me from complaining about it.

Getting rid of Dad whilst we put up the tree was another Christmas tradition that we started last year, after years of him taking the fun out of it. Mum always said that Christmas was about kids, and that included decorating the tree. Dad, on the other hand, always said that he didn't want a messy looking tree sitting in his lounge for a month, and if we were going to do it, then we had to do it properly.

By 'properly', he meant that decorations had to be colour co-ordinated in a combination of red and gold, and baubles had to be spaced a regimented five inches apart. Only traditional wooden, handmade decorations coloured in red and gold were allowed to accompany the baubles on the tree. And absolutely NO tinsel!

Watching Mum dancing across the lounge now with tinsel wrapped around her hair, I really did wonder sometimes how on earth they got married in the first place!

"Let's put this one at the top," said Little Spud, as he scrambled onto the arm of the sofa, trying to reach the top of the tree. Mum managed to get an arm around his little waist just in time before he toppled into the tree itself. Dad would have spontaneously combusted if he'd witnessed what had just happened. Little Spud giggled as Mum caught him, waving the random cardboard cut-out with glitter over it in her face.

"That's nice sweetheart," Mum said to him, "let's put it right here so we can all see it."

Mum proceeded to dangle the bizarre looking Christmas decoration that Little Spud had made at pre-school on one of the branches to the right of the tree.

Pocket Rocket and I exchanged a knowing glance as he quickly removed the decoration from where Mum had just hung it. He then positioned it at a slightly less prominent angle – otherwise known as the back of the tree where no one could see it!

Mum always made a huge fuss about

the Christmas decorations that my brothers and I had made when we were younger. She said that we were making memories. Hanging a piece of cardboard covered in glitter on the tree was just taking things a bit too far though.

An hour (and far too many cheesy Christmas songs) later, Mum carefully placed the traditional star at the top of the tree.

It glistened brightly as the fairy lights shone up at it. We all stood back to marvel at our creation.

"I'd say that's our best effort yet, boys," said Mum. "I reckon even Dad would struggle to find fault with that."

“Now for the best bit!” shouted Big Spud as he ran into the kitchen. He grabbed a packet of Father Christmas shaped chocolates from the worktop, and ran back to the tree as fast as his little legs would carry him. He was about to tip all of them out onto the sofa when Mum quickly snatched the packet from him.

“Not so fast mister!” she said. “You lot go into the hallway and count to twenty, whilst I hide four chocolates on the tree for you to find.”

“Ooh, I can count to twenty,” grinned Little Spud as he led the way out into the hallway. “Oneee, twooo, threee, fourrr, fiveee,” he slurred.

“Hurry up Little Spud,” moaned Big Spud. “Count quicker or Mum will eat all the chocolates!”

Little Spud didn’t like the sound of that. He sped up his counting as we all waited impatiently. “Six, seven, eight, nine, ten, eleventeen, twelveteen...”

"That's not even a number," laughed Pocket Rocket.

"Yes it is!" exclaimed Little Spud, looking offended. "Let me finish! Thirteen, sixteen, seventeen, twenteen."

That was good enough for us. Pocket Rocket, Big Spud and I shouted "twenteen" in unison, much to the delight of our youngest brother who now thought his version of "twenty" was the correct one.

We ran back into the lounge, and charged over to the Christmas tree like we were competing in a one-hundred-metre sprint.

"Found one!" shouted Pocket Rocket, as he grabbed a chocolate from a branch near the bottom of the tree. He caused a dusting of pine needles to drop to the floor in his haste. Every year, Mum would sweep up pine needles at the end of the day, whilst muttering something about getting an artificial tree the following year. She always seemed to forget by the next Christmas though, as we would all traipse to the local garden centre to choose our tree. We would then tie it on to the roof of the car to bring it home.

This was always an exciting trip out as it meant that the countdown to Christmas was well and truly underway. An artificial tree wouldn't have the same smell to it either. I have always loved the fresh, sweet smell of pine that drifts up into my nostrils as I walk into the room. It also acts as a very handy air freshener when Pocket Rocket takes his socks off!

"Erm, just the one chocolate, Pocket Rocket," scolded Mum as he continued to look for another one on the tree. "Give your brothers a chance."

Pocket Rocket slumped down on the sofa looking disgruntled, as he peeled the wrapper from his one lonely chocolate.

I was the next to find mine. It was buried deep in the middle of the tree, hanging behind a wooden figure of an elf wrapping a red present with a gold bow.

Big Spud found his shortly afterwards, as he stood on the edge of the sofa and stretched his little arm up as high as he could. Clumsily, he tugged on the tiny gold cord that hung the chocolate from the tree. Mum tutted as more pine needles fell silently to the floor.

"S'not fair," groaned Little Spud. "I didn't get one."

"There's still one more hiding," said Mum. "Do you want your brothers to help you?"

"No," he replied indignantly. He was so stubborn sometimes. "Do cold and shivery."

"Do you mean 'hot and cold?" I asked him.

"Yep, that!"

"OK," said Mum as Little Spud moved his podgy arm slowly across the tree.

"Cold, cold, warmer, warm, hot, boiling hot, cold again."

Dramatically, I slapped my hand to my forehead. This could go on forever! Ten minutes later, after Mum had lost the will to live, Little Spud finally found his Father Christmas chocolate, hanging in between a glittery red bauble and a shiny gold star.

He cheered like he had won the lottery when finally he had it in his hands. Just then, Dad walked through the front door with Obi and Lola.

"Not bad," he said nodding his head as he appraised the newly decorated tree. "Boys, it would seem you have finally learnt the art of tree decorating, except for maybe one little tweak here," he said, moving a gold bauble one branch to the left. "And maybe one little tweak there."

He was about to move another decoration when we all shouted, "Daaaaad!"

"OK, OK," he relented. "I'll leave it alone." He winked at Mum. My brothers were oblivious to it, but being the eldest, I knew that the wink meant that he would wait until we were all fast asleep tonight. He would then make a few 'little' adjustments to make the tree 'perfect', and hope that none of us noticed.

"Anyway," he said, "I have something to show you." He opened up the local newspaper that he was holding under his arm and started reading...

"Could you be the next big news reporter? Write a report on anything related to Christmas, and enter our competition to not only win £50 prize money, but also have your story printed on the front page! Open to all children aged seven to eleven years old!"

I tickled Obi and Lola behind their ears, as I listened intently to Dad. £50 prize money for writing a news report! My eyes grew wide as I thought how many chocolate bars I would need to sell at my secret school tuck shop to make just £10, let alone £50! Only last week, I had received a silver award at school for a report that I had written. It was about the inter-school karate tournament. It would have been a gold award, but apparently, according to Miss Leggit, the head of P.E., the joke that I had added in was "insensitive" and "mean". The kids at school didn't seem to think so though. The entire hall had erupted into laughter when I described Harry Boyce screeching like an angry chimpanzee whenever he did his kiai. I didn't mean to embarrass him, and I made it up to him by giving him a private kiai lesson in the playground the following lunch time. I had developed his kiai from a screeching chimpanzee to a fearsome hyena.

I was going for fearsome lion, but would settle for hyena for the time being. I'm not a miracle worker you know! If I could entertain the kids at school with a report about a karate tournament, then surely I could write about something Christmassy! I had this in the bag. That prize money was as good as mine!

(Kiai – the name given to the shout someone makes when performing an attacking move in karate.)

CHAPTER 3

"So what are you going to write about, Ben?" asked my best friend, Tommy, referring to my latest money making plan to win the newspaper competition. We were sitting in the school hall, eating our lunch, two days later. The smell of sweaty feet mixed with overcooked broccoli lingered around us, making my lungs crave the fresh air of the playground. Parents were invited in to have lunch with us a few months back, and Mum said how it had smelt exactly the same in her school lunch hall when she was a child. According to her, the food they served nowadays was much better, although I have to admit, I found this very hard to believe. As she had devoured her dry chocolate cake for pudding, she had said that a jam roly-poly was as good as it got in her day.

"I'm not too sure yet," I replied to his question. It was actually harder than I thought to decide what to do. "It needs to be perfect though. There's no way I'm going to mess this up, and miss out on winning that £50 prize money."

"Win £50 for what?" came an annoying voice from behind me. Nosey Natalie was walking past us with her dinner tray and her ears had pricked up at the sound of our conversation.

"I didn't say anything about winning £50," I said quickly. The last thing I wanted was for Nosey Natalie to hear about the competition. The whole school would know by the end of the day, and that would only mean one thing – more competition, and therefore less chance of winning.

Tommy quickly backed me up. "You mean 50p Natalie, not £50!"

Natalie squinted her eyes at us suspiciously. "You definitely said £50," she said, "I heard you!"

"Nope, definitely 50p," I lied. "Tommy and I are having a little bet on something. If Tommy wins, I have to give him 50p, and if

I win, he has to give me 50p. Right Tommy?"

"Right Ben," Tommy nodded.

"So what is the bet then?" asked Nosey Natalie, raising her eyebrows upwards.

Tommy and I looked at each other for a second as we racked our brains. Suddenly, I spotted a dinner lady who we all called 'Sarge' behind her back. She earned herself this nickname due to the fact that she was on a total power trip. She bossed kids around left, right, and centre like she was a Sergeant Major, and we were her army recruits.

"I bet Tommy that before I finish eating this lump of broccoli, Sarge would have shouted at some poor kid for not eating every last mouthful of their putrid mush of soggy pasta. If I'm right, he has to give me 50p, and if I'm wrong I have to give him 50p."

"That sounds fun, can I bet too?" asked Nosey Natalie.

"Erm, OK," I agreed reluctantly as she put her dinner tray down opposite mine and took a seat. Oh for crying out loud, now I would actually have to eat the poor excuse for broccoli. I had planned on sneakily tipping it into the bin when the dinner ladies had their backs turned. I could have really done with Obi and Lola sneaking under the table right then to gobble it out of my hand.

"Go on then," said Nosey Natalie impatiently. "It's cheating if you take too long to eat the broccoli!"

"She's right," joined in Tommy. "You'd better get eating Ben, or the bet's off!" He smirked at me, enjoying every second of my discomfort.

Glaring at him, I dug my fork into the

soggy piece of broccoli that lay on my plate. It looked like a miniature tree that had been cut down a year ago and left to rot.

As I lifted it towards my lips, the smell of it hit my nostrils and I had to fight the urge to gag. It smelt like cat vomit mixed with Pocket Rocket's stinky socks. I was about to open my lips and sink my teeth into the monstrosity on my fork when I heard Sarge's voice booming through the lunch hall.

"You boy, get back in your seat with that tray RIGHT NOW!" she shouted.

I looked up and saw a poor boy from year one called Alfie literally shaking as he realised he had been caught. His attempt to perform the ultimate sin of not eating every last mouthful of his school dinner had been thwarted by none other than Sarge herself.

"I want to see every last mouthful of that pasta eaten by the time I count to twenty," she boomed. "ONE...TWO...THREE..."

Poor Alfie started to eat mouthfuls of his sloppy pasta as quickly as he could, whilst feeling the burn of hundreds of pairs of eyes on him. Everyone else in the lunch hall watched him, feeling thankful that they weren't the ones under Sarge's fire right then. She was a menacing looking woman, if indeed she was a woman, as quite frankly she could have been a man wearing a dress for all I knew. She was so tall that she had to duck her head down as she walked through the door into the kitchen. She looked about fifty years old, and always had her grey hair scraped back into a tight bun on the top of her head. This just accentuated the mass of double, no actually triple, on second thoughts make that quadruple, chins that she had hanging round her neck.

I put my piece of broccoli back down on my plate and held out my left hand to Tommy. Then my right hand to Nosey Natalie.

"I think you'll find that you owe me 50p

each, thank you very much," I said smugly.

"That's not fair, you cheated," whined Nosey Natalie.

"I won fair and square, Natalie," I replied. "Right, Tommy?"

I knew that Tommy would back me up. He was my best friend for one, and secondly, 50p was nothing to him when his millionaire Dad gave him £50 to spend on snacks every day!

"Fine," said Nosey Natalie as she stood up in a strop. "But you still have to eat the broccoli, or no deal."

"She's right, Ben, I'm afraid. You did say 'before you have eaten the broccoli,' and technically that means that you still have to eat it."

They were correct of course, and I hated to have my integrity under fire. I had to man up and eat the broccoli! Holding my nose, I opened my mouth wide and bit the whole lot off of the stalk in one go.

My cheeks actually hurt as the horrendous flavour covered my taste buds. My obvious discomfort seemed to please Nosey Natalie as she stood up and told me she would give me the 50p later.

She sauntered off to a table of girls nearby. As I watched her, I thought to myself that never in a million years would Nosey Natalie pay her debt. I didn't care, though. I had bigger and better things to worry about, like winning the competition in the newspaper and bagging myself the £50 prize money.

CHAPTER 4

"Muuuuuuuum!"

The following morning, I woke up to the sound of Pocket Rocket shouting for Mum at the top of his voice. I rubbed my sleepy eyes, and reached down to stroke Obi who was curled up at the end of my bed as usual. I crawled down my duvet so that I could lie next to him, and snuggled my head into the soft fur on his tummy. Maybe just five more minutes sleep.

"Muuuuuuuuum, come here quickly!" Pocket Rocket shouted even louder this time. I groaned as I realised my five minutes more sleep was not going to happen with my noisy brother around. I heard Mum's footsteps walking down the stairs to see what drama could possibly be so important this early in the morning. I grabbed my dressing gown from the end of my bed, and followed her down to see what all the fuss was about.

I was greeted in the kitchen by Pocket Rocket holding up his advent calendar. Every single one of the doors had been ripped open. Shiny silver foil hung in big patches where bite-sized chocolates had once sat.

I took one look at Little Spud hiding under the kitchen table, and put two and two together. It certainly didn't take a genius to work out what had happened.

"Little Spud has eaten my entire advent calendar!" wailed Pocket Rocket. He charged at the kitchen table and made a grab for our naughty little brother. He would have got him too, if Mum hadn't stepped between them just in time.

"Hang on a minute," she said. "How do

you know it was Little Spud? It could have been Obi or Lola for all we know."

Seeing his chance to hide behind 'Mummy,' Little Spud crawled out from under the table.

"Yeah," he said, "I bet it was Lola!"

We all looked at Little Spud in disbelief as he said this.

"OK," I said. "And if Lola did this, do you think she would have chocolate all around her face, Little Spud."

"Yep," he replied smugly, and then thought for a moment. "But she's probably licked it all off by now."

Mum raised one of her eyebrows at Little Spud, and gave him the 'mum-look-of-disappointment.'

"Come with me, and look in the mirror," she said to him.

She picked Little Spud up and carried him into the lounge. My brothers and I followed her to see our youngest brother get busted.

As he looked in the mirror, Little Spud saw a face looking back at him that seemed just like his, only this one had chocolate smeared all over it.

"Lola must have licked me after she ate all of the locolate," he exclaimed.

Wow, he was pretty impressive for a three year old! He may not be able to say 'chocolate' properly yet, but he was very good at being devious.

"Little Spud, I am so cross with you," Mum said, as she put him down on the floor. She knelt down in front of him so that her eyes were at the same level as his. Ooh, wait for it, wait for it, she's going for the 'I'm so disappointed in you' speech for sure!

"No actually, I'm not cross, I'm disappointed in you, which is much worse," she continued.

And boom, there you have it. Mums are so predictable.

"How could you eat an entire advent calendar just a few days into December? And you didn't even eat your own. You took your brother's which is even worse."

"Yeah Spud," chimed in Pocket Rocket.

"You are going to give your advent calendar to your brother, and you are going to have to go without one for the whole of December," Mum told him.

"You can't do that," wailed Little Spud.

"Father Christmas won't know when to come if I don't have a badvent cawendar."

Big Spud started laughing at this point. "Haha, yours is a 'badvent' calendar now Little Spud," he said in a singsong voice. "You're bad and Father Christmas is bringing you a lump of coal."

This was just too much for Little Spud.

"Nooooo," he wailed. "Sowwy Mum, sowwy Pocket Rocket. Pwease don't tell Farver Kissmas, pwease!"

I almost felt sorry for the little devil.

"Alright, alright," said Mum. "Calm down. If you promise that you really have learnt your lesson, I will give you one more chance. And from now on, it won't be me that tells Father Christmas if you're naughty. It will be this elf that he sent me yesterday."

She went over to a cupboard in the kitchen, and pulled out the freakiest looking toy elf I had ever seen. It was dressed entirely in red, including a big pointy red hat. It had a smug looking face with big round, sneaky, blue eyes.

"This boys, is Elvis the elf. He has come to keep an eye on you so that Father Christmas knows whether or not you deserve to get presents this year."

"Don't be silly Mum," said Pocket Rocket. "It's just a doll."

"It may look like a doll," said Mum, "but trust me, Elvis is very real, and he will see everything that you boys do, and I mean EVERYTHING!"

Big Spud and Little Spud looked terrified at that. I had to give Mum credit for this one. She was good. Bringing a pretend elf into the house to get her sons to behave. Genius! Come to think of it, maybe I could write a newspaper report about it for the competition. The headline would read...

"MUM WINS IN BATTLE TO MAKE KIDS BEHAVE WITH A LITTLE HELP FROM A FAKE ELF"

I could almost feel the £50 prize money in my hand. This was sure to win me the competition.

CHAPTER 5

Pah, so much for the fake elf story winning me the competition. Four days later, and my headline would now have to read something like this...

"NOT SO FAKE ELF MEETS A STICKY END AS KIDS WIN AGAINST MUM!"

Everything was going great for the first day. Elvis had been sitting nice and still on the window sill in the lounge, minding his own business. Big Spud and Little Spud had been going over and poking him in the tummy every now and then to test whether he was real. Then, when they got no response, they would go and report back to Mum that he wasn't saying 'ouch' when they poked him, so he must just be a doll.

Mum would then tell them not to be mean to him, and that he was under strict orders from Father Christmas to pretend to be a doll when children were around. Only when they were fast asleep at night was he allowed to come alive. Pocket Rocket and I had laughed at the time, thinking how gullible our little brothers were to believe this.

That all changed the first morning after Elvis came to stay though. I was awoken to shrieks from Big Spud and Little Spud in the bathroom. I shouted out to them to be quiet which made them squeal even more. They were saying something about Elvis and toothpaste. I reached out to tickle Obi behind his ears as I dragged my sleepy head out of bed. In the bathroom, I spotted Elvis the elf sitting on the edge of the sink, holding our tube of toothpaste. The mirror above him had the word 'Boo!' smeared on it in toothpaste.

"Look Ben," squealed Little Spud happily. "He's a naughty elf, like me. That means I can be naughty too, and he won't tell Father Christmas."

Mum suddenly appeared in the bathroom. "Oh no it doesn't mister," she said quickly. "Just because Elvis is naughty, that doesn't mean you can be naughty together. He will still tell Father Christmas about you."

Little Spud crossed his arms and huffed, "Well, then I'll tell Father Christmas about him too!" he said indignantly.

"But Elvis isn't the one who needs to be good to get presents from Father Christmas," said Mum logically. "He just helps make the presents, remember?"

Little Spud looked defeated. "OK," he said moodily. "S'not fair though."

He glared at the elf sitting motionless on the sink and stormed out of the bathroom.

I looked suspiciously at the elf, and then at Mum. She muttered what a naughty elf he was, making more work for her as she began to wipe the mirror to get rid of the toothpaste.

I was convinced that he was a fake elf,

but if that was true, then who put him in the bathroom and wrote 'Boo!' on the mirror? At this stage, I was still thinking it would make a good article for the newspaper. But first, I had to find out a bit more about how this whole fake elf spy thing worked. I knew it wasn't Mum making it up, as she always moaned about cleaning up after us around the house. That meant there was no way in the world she would put toothpaste on the mirror just to have to clean it off again. That would be ridiculous. There was only one explanation. It had to be Dad.

That theory however, was completely destroyed the following morning when we woke up to Elvis' latest antics. Mum told us to creep quietly into her bedroom with her where Dad was still asleep. Elvis was sitting on the end of their bed with Mum's bright pink nail varnish resting on his lap. One arm was hugging tightly onto it, whilst the other was resting on the lid. We all looked down at Dad's feet poking out of the end of the duvet, and saw that his toenails were all bright pink. Elvis had only gone and painted Dad's toenails whilst he was sleeping!

My brothers squealed with delight when they saw what the naughty elf had done. Quickly, Mum ushered them out of the room before they could wake Dad up. The damage was done though. We all ran down the stairs to the sound of Dad shouting, "What on earth has happened to my toes?"

It would have been funny if it hadn't been for the fact that I knew that Dad wouldn't have painted his own toenails bright pink. Therefore, it couldn't have been him behind the fake elf. There could only be one explanation. The elf had to be real!

I didn't like this one bit. The next night, Elvis took all of the marshmallows out of the cupboard and made an igloo out of them to sleep in.

This really bugged me, as it wasted a whole lot of marshmallows that could have gone into my hot chocolate.

The final straw came a day later though, when I woke up to find Lola with a big bald stripe down her back. Elvis was sitting on the kitchen table with the dog clippers in his arms. Guilty!

I grabbed hold of Elvis, quickly checked no one was looking, and ran out of the front door with him. This freaky dude was getting out of my house the fastest way possible. I ran five doors down to where a little girl called Alice lived and left the elf on her doorstep. I rang the doorbell and then ran back to my house as fast as I could. It was time for this mischievous elf to spy on someone else for Father Christmas. I would just tell my brothers that Elvis had received a phone call from Father Christmas to tell him he was needed back at the North Pole straight away to start wrapping presents for Christmas Eve.

Elvis has left the building!

CHAPTER 6

"So this year, we will be doing a Christmas show with a difference," Mr Growler finally concluded after what had felt like an hour of him rambling on about the true meaning of Christmas.

I was sitting in the school hall, listening to the usual boring Friday morning assembly from my headmaster, Mr Growler. My bottom felt numb where it was probably getting frost bite from sitting on the cold hard floor for so long. I shifted uncomfortably as I tried not to nudge my classmate Olivia who was sitting next to me. My teacher this year, Miss Jackson, insisted on sitting us boy, girl, boy, girl. It was so annoying when teachers did controlling things like that. It could be worse though. At least I was sitting between Olivia and another girl called Lexi. Poor Tommy had got stuck between Evil Emily and Nosey Natalie. How unlucky could you get?

My ears pricked up at the sound of 'a Christmas show with a difference.' Usually, each year group did their own Christmas play based around the story of the baby Jesus. There were only so many times you could dress up as a wise man and get enthusiastic about it! I don't think I could have faced doing it again this year.

"This year," continued Mr Growler, "the entire school will do one show together!"

An excited murmur erupted amongst the children all around me. This was quickly hushed by the teachers sitting around the edge of the school hall like marshals, making sure no one stepped out of line.

"Of course, we will still have the traditional Christmas story of baby Jesus in there," Mr Growler went on, "but we will also have some more modern Christmas songs, some street dancing as you kids call it, and the teachers will be getting involved too."

A few kids cheered at this point, as they undoubtedly pictured their teachers completely humiliating themselves as they tried to sing and dance. Once again, the 'marshals' hushed the trouble-makers.

"You'll be practising in your year groups over the next few weeks," said Mr Growler. "Then we will all come together for a few big rehearsals before showing your parents the best Christmas show Summercroft School has ever done!"

Almost the entire room cheered at this point. After a failed attempt to shush everyone for a third time, the teachers gave up and allowed everyone to exit the hall, cheering and chattering which was unusual for a school assembly. I caught up with Tommy as he walked back to our classroom slightly ahead of me.

"Have you come up with any more ideas for the newspaper report?" he asked.

"Nope," I answered, raising my eyebrows. I was really struggling to think of something.

"How about you write about the switching on of the Christmas lights tonight?" Tommy suggested. "They're bound to have someone famous turning them on."

Tommy was right. The town centre always made a big deal about switching on the Christmas lights. That could be my winning story!

CHAPTER 7

"Hurry up Mum, I want to get there early so that I can get an interview with Leo!"

Leo Sparks was the local celebrity tasked with the job of switching on the Christmas lights in front of hundreds of excited people. He was the author of the latest children's book, 'How To Trick Your Teacher', that all the kids at school were talking about, and the fact that he was here in our town was awesome.

"OK, I'm coming," Mum replied. "I just need to find the socks that Little Spud just took off."

Urgh, why did my little brother always have to undress himself when we were trying to go somewhere?

Ten minutes later, after Little Spud had finished having a tantrum about the fact that his socks were light blue and not dark blue, we left the house.

“I’ll drive,” said Dad, snatching the keys from Mum.

“I’m quite capable,” said Mum.

“Hmm, tell that to the poor paint-work on the car door,” said Dad sarcastically.

He was referring to the scrapes down the side of the car that Mum had caused by getting the car stuck between two bushes yesterday. She had misjudged the width of her friend’s driveway when she’d tried to park in it, and had found herself completely wedged in between two rows of bushes that were more thorny branches than beautiful flowers.

She literally had to call Dad to come round with his chainsaw to cut the bushes back so that she could dislodge the car!

Mum went to open her mouth to defend herself, but quickly closed it again when she realised that she didn't have a leg to stand on at that moment in time. She busied herself strapping Little Spud into his car seat, ignoring our sniggers as we all pictured her trapped inside the car.

"Maybe we should get a car with a sunroof next time, Mum," suggested Pocket Rocket. "That way, you can just climb through the roof when you get the car stuck again."

"Well aren't you a little comedian," replied Mum sarcastically. "Do your strap up before I eject you through the sunroof myself!"

"But we don't have one Mum," chimed in Big Spud. "Remember? That's why you couldn't climb out of the car when you got stuck in the bushes."

"Alright, enough about my little mishap," said Mum in an exasperated voice. "Everyone makes mistakes from time to time. Now let's get going before we miss the Christmas lights being turned on."

Tommy was with us too of course. His parents had never taken him to see the switching on of the Christmas lights before, so Mum was more than happy for him to come with us. He squeezed into the car in the middle of Big Spud and Little Spud. They grinned happily when they realised that they had both got their way in their demands to sit next to Tommy. Pocket Rocket and I climbed into the seats at the back of the car, and Mum and Dad climbed into the front – with Dad in the driving seat.

After driving round the car park several times trying to find a parking space, we quickly walked to the high street. Big Spud and Little Spud couldn't keep up, so Mum and Dad ended up giving them piggybacks.

My annoying little brothers didn't make this easy as they kept smacking their bottoms, trying to make them gallop like horses. I swear Mum was tempted to drop Little Spud off in a bin at one point.

As we got nearer to the high street, we heard music blaring out of what must have been enormous speakers. A local dance crew came into view on a stage that had been set up just for tonight. I craned my neck, trying to catch a glimpse of where Leo

Sparks might be. I had my notepad and pen firmly rooted in my hand, waiting for just the right moment.

"Don't forget to write down things like how the atmosphere is here, and all the extra bits like how there's a dance crew," advised Tommy.

He was right. I was so focused on getting an interview with Leo, that I had forgotten that I needed to put down everything else that went into writing a good newspaper report. Tommy and I had looked it up on the internet the other day by googling 'how to write a good newspaper article.' Apparently, the essential information needed was Who, What, Where, When, Why and How. Just writing those things wasn't going to make me stand out, though. I needed to give it a little something extra. I needed some quotes from Leo himself. That was sure to be worthy of front-page news, and win the competition.

Suddenly, I heard a girl in front of me

shout, "There he is!" as she pointed to the steps to the left of the stage. There must have been at least a thousand people standing around us. How on earth would I get through all of these crowds to interview Leo and get the perfect scoop?

Shouting to Mum that I would be back in five minutes, I grabbed Tommy by his arm and we started jostling our way through everyone to get closer to the front of the stage. We had a few disgruntled 'oi's' moaned at us, and also an 'ouch' when I accidentally stood on an old lady's foot. This was no time for pleasantries though. A good reporter had to get his story at all costs. We had almost made it when Leo started to make his way further up the steps and onto the stage.

"Leo," I shouted.

He ignored me.

"LEO," I shouted again, a little louder this time.

He ignored me again.

"LEO," Tommy yelled in a voice that sounded like it belonged to a six foot, three inch tall WWE wrestler weighing 286 pounds, rather than a small ten-year-old boy.

The entire crowd seemed to turn to look at us, including Leo Sparks! I stared at him, speechless for a second, until Tommy nudged me in the back. I mustered up the biggest voice I could, feeling a little silly now that everyone was looking at me.

"Erm, can I get an interview with you

please?" I said, waving my notebook and pen at him.

"Sure kid, no problem," he replied. "Come to the stage steps about 7.00pm after I've pressed this big switch here."

He indicated towards a big red button that sat on top of a table on the stage. It looked a bit cheap and plastic up close. Surely they should at least have a gold coloured button for something as important as switching on the Christmas lights!

I looked at Tommy, not quite believing my luck. Before I could say anything, I heard Leo's voice coming out loud and clear through the speakers.

"Good evening Guildford!" he boomed into the microphone.

"Good evening Leo," chorused the people of Guildford town, who had come to watch this momentous occasion of the Christmas lights being turned on.

"Are you all enjoying my book, kids?" Leo shouted once more.

A deafening shout of "Yes!" came out from the audience. One smart-aleck kid waited for the noise to die down before shouting "No", trying to be funny. There was always one! *I hope it wasn't Pocket Rocket,* I suddenly thought, not daring to turn around to check.

Ignoring the heckler, Leo started the countdown as everyone joined in. "Ten, nine, eight, seven, six, five, four, three, two, one, Merry Christmas!

A big cheer went up as the Christmas lights overhead emblazoned into action. Gold and red confetti mixed with fake snow shot out of cannons surrounding the stage, covering everyone within reach.

'Oh I wish it could be Christmas every day,' by Wizard blasted out of the speakers, as everyone over the age of thirty-five sang along. Thanks to Mum insisting on putting on all the old cheesy Christmas songs whilst we decorated the Christmas tree, I could have sung along word for word too... if I had wanted to... which of course I didn't.

It was impossible not to get swept up in the excitement of it all. Christmas really was coming! Tommy and I weaved our way through the crowds back to Mum and Dad before they got worried about losing us. We made it back just as the song finished, saving us the trauma of hearing Mum singing along. She literally had the worst singing voice I had ever heard. I honestly ran downstairs one day thinking that Obi had shut his tail in a door, only to find Mum screeching along to her Whitney Houston album.

"Hi boys," she said, smiling. Mum loved

Christmas time. “Isn’t this fantastic!”

“Yeah, it’s great,” replied Tommy enthusiastically. I had forgotten that this was his first time seeing the Christmas lights turned on.

“Mum, I just need to go and interview Leo. He said to meet him by the stage at 7.00pm and it’s 6.55pm now.”

“Oh wow, how exciting,” exclaimed Mum. “Do you want us all to come?”

I didn’t need long to mull this one over. ‘No, no, no, no, no, absolutely not, no way in the world would I want my family embarrassing me’... is what I said in my head.

To Mum, I simply said, “No thanks, we won’t be long,” as I once again grabbed Tommy’s arm and barged my way through the crowd back to the stage. I was about to get my exclusive interview that would win me the competition. I couldn’t wait!

It was as I reached the bottom of the stage steps that the reality hit me. Standing three steps up was Leo Sparks. Standing three steps down were twenty-five other kids, all waving notepads and pens. It looked like I wasn't the only one who had heard about the newspaper competition to write an article connected to Christmas. So much for my exclusive interview! Apparently, the turning on of the Christmas lights was far from an original scoop after all!

CHAPTER 8

"Come on children, we haven't got all day," moaned Mrs Jackson as she ushered us into our seats.

It was now a week since my failed attempt to get my exclusive interview with Leo Sparks, and I was running out of ideas for the newspaper article. It was looking like I would end up having to do it about something lame like the Christmas play. I would have to make it stand out in some way though, as I was sure lots of other kids would be writing about their Christmas performances, too. Mr Growler had better be right about this being the best Christmas show Summercroft School had ever done! No one was going to be interested in reading about the traditional nativity story on the front page of the newspaper, that was for sure. The public wanted news that was going to shock them. They wanted a headline that was going to make them turn their heads as they walked past the newspaper stand on their way to the fruit and veg aisle. Could my school show provide such a captivating headline? I seriously doubted it, but it was all I had to work with at that moment in time.

Earlier in the week, we had all put our ideas forward for the contribution of our class to the show. Mrs Jackson had narrowed it down to the three best ideas, and this morning, we voted for our favourite. Once we were all seated, she was going to announce the winner.

There was a feeling of excitement amongst everyone in the class. We were all eager to hear the winning suggestion. The three shortlisted ideas came from a boy called Max, a girl called Amber, and none other than my best friend Tommy. It will come as no surprise to you that I voted for Tommy, of course. Even if he hadn't had the best idea, I still would have voted for him, as that's what best friends do. The fact that he did have, in my opinion, the best idea ever, was just a bonus.

The room was silent except for the sound of one of the other boys in my class, Zayan, tapping his hands on his desk in a drum roll. For once, Mrs Jackson took a break from being in strict, bossy teacher mode, as she let him continue with the drum roll to create a bit of atmosphere.

"And the winner is..." She paused for dramatic effect as we all sat there, wide-eyed, waiting to hear. There was silence for what seemed like ages. And then... "Tommy!"

A cheer went up around the class. Tommy's cheeks tinged red with embarrassment, but the smile that he couldn't stop from appearing on his lips showed how chuffed he was. Apart from running the secret school tuck shop with me, Tommy was quite a quiet kid at school. He came across as a bit shy until you got to know him. I had definitely got to know the real Tommy after spending hours up in his tree house with him. He was actually really funny. Something the other kids were now seeing as so many of them voted for his idea.

"Well, it looks like our contribution to the school Christmas show really will make it a performance with a difference this year, kids," announced Mrs Jackson, looking slightly worried. "This year, class 6J will do a five minute interpretation of the Christmas Nativity... in the style of the Home Alone movie!"

A cheer once again went up in the classroom, as we all imagined how much fun this was going to be.

"I'm not entirely sure how we're going to

do this," went on Mrs Jackson, "but I'm sure you will all have some great ideas. And with that, I want you all to write this week's homework in your homework diaries."

A collective groan went out as everyone was brought back to the boring reality of homework. Our groans were soon replaced with happy gasps of surprise, though, when Mrs Jackson told us to write word for word what she was saying... "Homework – Watch the *Home Alone* movie to get your imaginations working!"

If only all homework was that much fun!

CHAPTER 9

"Why don't we have a family movie night?" said Mum when I told her about my homework. "Christmas is only a few weeks away, so it's about time we started our Christmas movie nights."

We often had a movie night on a Friday, but leading up to Christmas we seemed to have even more than usual as Mum got us into the spirit of Christmas with movies like *Elf, The Polar Express,* and of course, *Home Alone.* This had been a firm favourite of Pocket Rocket and mine for a few years now. Last time we watched it, Pocket Rocket had laughed so much that he'd fallen off the sofa and dropped his bowl of popcorn all over the floor. Obi and Lola had very kindly helped him clear it up with their big greedy tongues!

“Yay, movie night,” cheered Big Spud, overhearing our conversation.

“Yay, poppycorn and locolate,” joined in Little Spud.

Mum smiled and gave them both a big hug. “Yes, you can have poPCorn and CHocolate,” she said, laughing at Little Spud’s mispronunciation.

My little brother’s didn’t care which movie we watched on our movie nights, as long as Mum came up trumps with the movie snacks... which she always did without fail.

"Can Tommy come over for it too Mum?" I asked. "We could think of some ideas for our Christmas Play whilst we're watching it."

"Yes of course he can," replied Mum. "I'll get some extra munchies in."

Four hours later, Tommy and I were sitting on my bedroom floor, stuffed full of popcorn and chocolate after watching *Home Alone*. We had a notebook full of ideas for the Christmas Play. Most of them were Tommy's ideas if I'm being honest, but we did make a pretty good team.

"You should write a film script for a movie one day, Tommy," I said. "You're really good at this."

"Maybe I will," said Tommy, looking pleased with himself. "Ooh, I've got another one," he said, suddenly getting excited.

"How about King Herod keeps trying to sneak up on Mary and Joseph, but whenever he gets close, different farm animals sabotage him by setting booby traps for him."

"Um, I don't think King Herod was there at the birth of Jesus, Tommy," I said dubiously.

"It doesn't matter," he said. "It's called artistic license."

Satisfied with his justification, I nodded in agreement. This was the easiest homework EVER! I wasn't sure Mrs Jackson would approve of the idea, but at least we had one. And if she did agree, then I would definitely be putting my hand up to be a saboteur sheep this year!

CHAPTER 10

"Who wants to go to meet Father Christmas today?" said Dad in a big merry voice as he wandered into the kitchen the following Saturday morning. Mum was making pancakes as a treat, so we were all waiting eagerly at the table.

I thought for a second that Little Spud was going to topple from his chair in excitement.

"Me, me, me," he squealed.

"Will he have presents for us?" asked Big Spud with eyes as wide as saucers.

"Well that depends on whether you've been good boys," said Dad, clearly enjoying their excitement.

"We have been good!" they exclaimed in unison.

"Hmm, except for eating my friend's chocolates," piped up Mum from behind the pancake maker.

Pocket Rocket's eyes met mine as we

realised the first part of the mission, *Letter from Father Christmas,* had been put into action. I couldn't believe that the Spuds had literally taken the blame for that one. I almost felt sorry for them. I was about to tell Mum the truth about Pocket Rocket eating the chocolates when I felt a hard kick on my right shin.

I looked up to see Pocket Rocket mouthing something to me which looked like 'dogs' paws.' I pulled a face at him which was a combination of annoyance and pain from the leg kick mixed with sheer cluelessness.

Pocket Rocket rolled his eyes, and then said as quietly as he could through gritted teeth, “your chores... remember?”

‘Oh!’ I mouthed back to him, remembering that the ‘Father Christmas Letter’ also said that our little brothers had to do all of our chores for the whole of December! Maybe I didn’t need to tell Mum the truth right that second. I nodded my understanding to Pocket Rocket and pulled an imaginary zip across my lips to show him that his secret was safe... for the time being at least.

I drizzled a big dollop of syrup onto the pancake that Mum had just slid onto my plate.

“Yum, thanks Mum,” I said

“Hey, why does he get the first one?” moaned Pocket Rocket.

“Because,” said Mum, “he was the only one who said ‘please’ when I asked who wanted pancakes this morning!”

“I said please,” he grumbled back at her.

“No you didn’t,” said Mum. “If you remember, your exact words were, ‘Excellent idea charlady, now make it snappy!’ Which is why you are getting the last pancake rather than the first!”

“Can’t you take a joke?” said Pocket Rocket, folding his arms as he slunk back in his seat in defeat.

“This is delicious,” I said, feeling the need to wind my brother up even more. “The first pancakes are always the best.”

I looked smugly at my brother who was almost drooling as he watched me with big, jealous eyes.

It wasn't like he'd have to wait long. It literally took seconds to make each pancake on Mum's special pancake maker.

"So where are we going to meet Father Christmas then?" asked Mum, flashing me a look that spoke a thousand words, or more specifically the 'don't wind your brother up, I am really not in the mood for yet another brotherly bust up.'

"Apparently he'll be at the café at Heather Haven this afternoon," answered Dad. "I thought we could take the dogs for a walk and then see Father Christmas afterwards."

Heather Haven had once been my favourite place to walk the dogs. Obi and Lola could run for miles off of their leads without a road in sight. In between the paths there were huge patches of purple heather woven together. You had to make sure you stuck to the paths though, as there were snakes lurking deep within the heather. I had thought that Dad was just trying to scare us when he'd first told us about the adders – the only venomous snake in England. But then we actually saw one! I remember it as clearly as if it had happened yesterday. If Lottie, the girl who would one day be my girlfriend, asked me about it, the story would go...

'So one day, when I was walking the dogs at Heather Haven with Mum and my brothers, a snake came onto the path and reared its head up at us. I jumped in front of my brothers to protect them, grabbed the snake round the neck and single-handedly wrestled it to the ground as it tried to bite me with its ferocious fangs dripping with venom.'

In reality, the story went something a little more like this... 'So, one day, when I was walking the dogs at Heather Haven with my Mum and my brothers, a snake came onto the path and reared its head up at us. I screamed like a girl, and ran backwards towards Mum who was behind me on the path, trying to round up my three younger brothers who were walking at a snail's pace. I then stood there, shaking like a leaf, as Mum ran back towards the snake to get Obi and Lola who were about to pounce on it like it was a toy. Pocket Rocket then had to give me a piggyback to the car as I was too scared to put my feet down.'

Little Spud found it so exciting that he demanded Mum bought him a snake teddy from the café shop on the way out. I, on the other hand, accepted that snakes were a new phobia that I could add to my list along with pretty much every creepy-crawly and spider you could think of.

Although traumatised by this event, I knew that it was safe to go to Heather Haven today as it was a cold, drizzly December day. Adders only ever come out onto the paths to catch the warmth of the sun – something England was seriously lacking in winter. This thought made me think of Lottie Jones, my (girl)friend who moved to Australia earlier in the year. I wondered what Christmas would be like for her. Surely it wouldn't feel as special if you didn't cosy up in your warm house with the fire blazing on Christmas Eve. Last time I spoke to her, she told me that they were planning on going to the beach on Christmas Day!

"Go and get dressed as soon as you finish your pancakes, boys," said Mum, snapping me out of my daydream. "We don't want Father Christmas to run out of presents!"

CHAPTER 11

A few hours later, with two worn out dogs, and six pairs of soggy wellies, we ventured into the café at Heather Haven.

"I can't believe you made us walk the dogs BEFORE seeing Father Christmas, Mum," moaned Big Spud. "What if he's already left to go back to the North Pole to check up on the elves?"

"Well, if he has gone back to the North Pole, he's forgotten to take one of his reindeer with him," said Dad with a glint in his eye.

We all looked out of the window to where Dad was pointing. Standing by the fence next to the grotto was a rather bored looking donkey wearing pretend antlers.

"Wow, a real reindeer!" exclaimed Little Spud. "I think it's Rudolf."

"If it's Rudolf, then why isn't his nose red?" asked Big Spud smugly, as if he was a very wise older big brother who knew best.

"It's not even a reind..." began Pocket Rocket. He stopped mid-sentence as Mum glared at him, warning him not to spoil the magic for our little brothers.

Being the eldest, I showed Pocket Rocket how it was done.

"It could be Rudolf," I said to Little Spud. "I heard a rumour that his nose only glows red at night, but during the day it looks just like any other reindeer's nose."

"That's right," said Dad, playing along as he gave me a subtle wink.

Pocket Rocket looked at me like I had gone mad. He really needed to work on this big brother stuff.

"Let's go and see Father Christmas now!"

shouted Little Spud as he ran to the door on the other side of the café. The owners knew what they were doing making everyone walk through the café to get to and from the grotto. They must be entrepreneurs like me. Who wouldn't be able to resist one of their delicious looking cakes on their way past after visiting the grotto.

We all followed Little Spud to the door. His excitement was contagious. At ten years old, I was definitely far too grown up to be visiting Father Christmas in his grotto. Thankfully, I had little brothers to use as an excuse to get away with it.

As we walked through the door, it was literally like we had just entered the North Pole. It reminded me of *The Lion, the Witch, and the Wardrobe* – a book I had read last year, where the children entered the enchanting world of Narnia through the back of a wardrobe.

The pathway had been covered in fake

snow, and fairy lights glistened along each side amongst rows of plants. We had definitely done the right thing in walking the dogs first, as now there was no queue at all. All that stood between us and Father Christmas was two elves. Or rather, a very short lady, and her even shorter daughter who were dressed in elf costumes. They beamed big smiles at us, and welcomed us with their rosy pink cheeks, shaking a bucket full of money under our noses.

Pocket Rocket's eyes lit up as he reached his grabby hand into the bucket and pulled out a handful of coins. Big Spud then followed suit, giggling with delight as he saw that, in amongst the coins, he had managed to get a £5 note between his fingers.

Little Spud was just about to copy them when Dad quickly intervened.

"I'm really sorry," he said to the elves who were standing there speechless, looking flabbergasted.

"Put the money back, boys," Dad said sternly, as he grabbed Pocket Rocket and Big Spud's wrists and shook them over the bucket. Big Spud's grip loosened straight away, and we heard the tinkle of coins dropping back into the bucket. Pocket Rocket wasn't so quick to release his grip. Dad gave an embarrassed laugh through gritted teeth as he let go of Big Spud's hand so that he could prise apart Pocket Rocket's fingers.

"But why are you putting it back, Daddy?" asked Little Spud with a puzzled face. "It's from Father Christmas."

Another clattering of coins could be heard as Dad finally managed to wedge his fingers in between Pocket Rocket's.

"Sorry," Dad apologised again to the elves, looking embarrassed. "I think they got the wrong end of the stick."

He pulled out his wallet and gave each of us a pound coin. "You don't take money out of the bucket, boys. You PUT IT IN the bucket."

"Why?" asked Little Spud. "Is Father Christmas poor?"

"No," said Mum, coming to Dad's help as he put his head in his hands. "Father Christmas is helping to give money to charity. The rule is, we get to see him, if we put a bit of money in the bucket to go towards..." she looked at the side of the bucket, to try to find out which charity it was.

"The local donkey sanctuary," said the lady elf.

"There you go," said Mum. "The donkey sanctuary, boys. Maybe we should give a little bit more," she said, nudging Dad with her elbow.

Dad pulled a £10 note out of his wallet and dropped it into the bucket much to the delight of the elves. That should redeem us for my foolish brothers mistaking the charity bucket for a *'grab all you can, courtesy of Father Christmas'* bucket.

We were saved from any embarrassing small talk by a big "Hohoho" coming from behind the door of the grotto. It was actually a gazebo that had been decorated with fairy lights and had a door made up of lots of long strands of tinsel hanging down – not the big fluffy looking strips of tinsel, but the long wispy individual silver strips. They looked like long icicles, waiting to be parted by eager little hands in their quest to see the big man himself.

Smiling at us, obviously forgiving us for our earlier mistake, the elves stepped aside to allow us to enter. I let my little brothers race ahead of me. I was just as excited as they were, but I couldn't let anyone see that. I was ten, not five! Once we were all inside, it was a bit of a squash.

"Hohoho," said Father Christmas. "Your mum and dad have certainly got their hands full with all of you boys, haven't they?"

It was nothing we hadn't heard before. It

was certainly better than the "poor Mummy, having so many boys," that we sometimes heard from miserable old ladies in the supermarket. Depending on Mum's mood, she would either, smile sweetly at them and tell them how lucky she was, or she would look at them like she was about to try out my karate moves on them.

"Now, who's going to come to sit next to me on this chair, and tell me what they would like for Christmas?" Father Christmas asked. Big Spud and Little Spud suddenly hid behind Mum, feeling shy.

"Why don't you go first, Ben?" said Mum. "Show your brothers how it's done."

I went and sat on the chair next to Father Christmas. By chair, I actually meant a bale of hay that felt scratchy on the backs of my legs. As usual, I had insisted on wearing shorts, even though it was about zero degrees outside.

"Now what would you like for Christmas this year, young man," Father Christmas asked me.

"Um, I don't know," I said, feeling like a little kid again. "Maybe an Xbox for my bedroom."

Dad started having a spontaneous coughing fit at this moment. "Maybe you should ask Father Christmas for something a bit less extravagant," he said, in between coughs. "He does have a lot of children to give presents to."

"Yes I certainly do," chuckled Father Christmas. "Now why don't you go and help yourself to a present from the tub over there whilst I chat to your brothers." He indicated to a big tub wrapped with Christmas paper, overflowing with presents. I guess the Xbox had been a bit of a long shot.

"Me next," said Pocket Rocket.

"No, me!" shouted Big Spud.

"What about me, I'm the dinkiest," said Little Spud, thinking that he'd get his way if he turned the cuteness factor up a notch.

"How about you all come and chat to me together," suggested Father Christmas. "I'm sure you can all squeeze onto this very special chair."

My brothers all bundled onto the hay bale together. Dad grabbed Little Spud just in time as he almost toppled over the back, not realising this *'chair'* didn't come with a backrest.

"So, do you little tinkers have any questions you'd like to ask me?" said Father Christmas.

Uh-oh. He was going to regret saying that. The next fifteen minutes went something along the lines of this:

"Have you ever got stuck in a chimney?"

"Do you really have a naughty and nice list?"

"Have you seen Elvis the elf lately?"

"Dad tells us to leave you beer on Christmas Eve, but you shouldn't drink and drive, so can we just leave you milk this year so you don't crash your sleigh?"

"Why did you tell us that we had to take the blame for eating Mum's chocolate when it was actually..."

The barrage of questions was stopped at this point when Pocket Rocket, about to get rumbled, decided to distract everyone by focusing on Father Christmas' beard.

"Is this beard real?" he asked, jumping off the hay bale and rushing over to give it a little tug.

"Pocket Rocket, NO!" yelled Mum.

But it was too late. Pocket Rocket had pulled the beard from Father Christmas's chin, revealing a big band of elastic round the back of it. All you could hear was a huge gasp from my younger brothers.

"You're not the real Farter Kisstmas!" shouted Little Spud, getting his words even more jumbled than usual in his state of shock.

"You tricked us!" shrieked Big Spud.

"Right boys, time to go I think," said Mum in an unnaturally chirpy voice. "Thank you for your time, Father Christmas. We look forward to you visiting us on Christmas Eve."

As Father Christmas sat there looking dazed, Dad grabbed the Spuds, one under each arm, and ushered me and Pocket Rocket out of the grotto. We had just about made it out to the safety of the café when Pocket Rocket remembered they hadn't got their presents. He ran back, and before the fake Father Christmas knew what was happening, he had grabbed five presents out of the tub. “The dogs need one too,” he said cheekily before running back out.

“Why is nothing ever simple with you lot?” Mum asked as we left the café.

“It’s not our fault, Mum,” replied Pocket Rocket. “He was a fake! We should report him to the police.”

I would have joined in the conversation, but I was already planning a headline in my head.

"Father Christmas Imposter Cons Innocent Children at Popular Dog Walking Site."

Perhaps, this could be the one to win me the competition!

CHAPTER 12

"Hey, check out this guy on the local news," Dad called out from the lounge where he was watching television. We were having an afternoon at home after our disastrous visit to Father Christmas.

"This guy has been doing random acts of kindness all round town whilst dressed in a Father Christmas disguise."

"Maybe it's the real Father Christmas," piped up Big Spud.

"Or that fake one again from Heather Haven," said Pocket Rocket frowning.

I wandered into the lounge to see what they were all talking about. There was someone on the television screen in a Father Christmas outfit with sunglasses on – presumably so that no one could recognise him by his eyes.

The camera showed him waving at a crowd before running off down the road. A member of the public had filmed him on their phone as he had approached a group of four homeless people and given them a pair of cosy socks each and a drink of hot chocolate.

"Apparently, this guy has been doing random acts of kindness all week dressed as Father Christmas," said Dad, looking impressed.

"What a lovely person," said Mum, coming into the room. "I wonder who he is? Or she for that matter. It could be a man or a lady under that disguise."

"I wonder if he'll reveal himself just before Christmas," said Dad.

"These guys never show their faces, Dad. They get a thrill out of people wondering who they are," I replied.

"Maybe he just wants to do something nice," said Mum. "Christmas time does bring out the best in people after all."

"Which is why you should get me an Xbox for my room for Christmas," I said, trying to look angelic. "It's the nice, kind thing to do."

"Nice try, Ben," said Dad, raising his eyebrows at my opportunistic remark.

A big debate ensued as to why Christmas was more about giving to others than getting things yourself. I wasn't listening, though. Every other idea that I'd had for the newspaper article had been blown out of the water by this one. I was going to find out who this man (or women!) was, and reveal their secret identity. This had just taken the competition to a whole new level!

CHAPTER 13

"OK, class, this is it. Show time," said Mrs Jackson.

It was two weeks later – the night of our Christmas play. Astonishingly, Mrs Jackson had given Tommy's suggestion for sabotaging King Herod a big thumbs-up, saying it showed creative thinking. I didn't get my wish to be the sheep saboteur, though, as it proved to be a very popular position with my fellow classmates, and Mrs Jackson ended up having to draw names out of a hat for it. I knew I wouldn't get picked. I am definitely not lucky when it comes to things like that.

I climbed into my costume ready for my starring role. OK, in truth, it wasn't exactly the 'star' role, but it was a very vital part of the nativity story. I pulled the hood over my head, and adjusted the ears that were flopping on top. The material felt scratchy against my skin as I straightened the arms and legs. Why did school play costumes always have to be so uncomfortable?

I laughed at Tommy struggling to get into his costume as the tail swung back and forth. At least I had been given a better deal than poor Tommy. After allocating the roles of Mary, Joseph, and King Herod to the more budding actors or ultra-confident people in the class, the animal roles were allocated on a strictly 'pull it out of the hat and hope' principle. I had been given the front of the donkey. Tommy had the privilege of being the donkey's butt!

"Laugh all you like," grinned Tommy. "At least I don't have to give a piggy back to Evil Emily."

I pulled a face at my best friend. Of all the people to play Mary, Mrs Jackson had chosen Emily. Evil Emily. Otherwise known as my arch-enemy. Life could be so cruel sometimes.

"Are you any closer to finding out who the Father Christmas guy is yet?" asked Tommy, as he finished buttoning up his costume.

"Only in that I know it's definitely a man, and not a lady," I replied.

"How do you know that?"

"Because someone managed to get a photo of him the other day and if you look really closely you can see a bit of stubble where his fake beard has come loose," I replied.

In the past few weeks, our Father Christmas do-gooder had been a very busy man. He had been spotted doing the following...

- Putting coins in parking meters along the high street to stop people being caught by the parking attendant.

- Walking through the shopping centre, giving compliments to random people.

- Handing homemade chocolate brownies through the windows of parked police cars and ambulances.

- Taking special Christmas dog treats to the local RSPCA.

- Dancing (very badly!) to songs like *Can't Stop The Feeling* and *Uptown Funk* in the town centre, just to put smiles on faces.

I knew all of this as I had had the genius idea to ask Mum to set me up an Instagram account, allowing people to tag their photos with the hashtag #mysteryfatherchristmas. It was all part of my plan to write the winning article for the local newspaper. I knew that others kids would have the idea to write about him as well. The difference was, I would be the one to reveal his true identity, I was sure of it...

CHAPTER 14

The Christmas play went as you would expect for a school play. The highlights were the bits that weren't meant to happen – little Holly from reception getting so excited when she saw her mum and dad in the audience that she literally peed her pants whilst waving at them, Timothy from Year Three singing 'Little Donkey' so loudly (and badly!) that even the grandad who had fallen fast asleep in the front row jolted awake. Oh and of course, Big Spud who never fails to entertain! He was part of the 'super cool' wise men crew, dressed complete with sunglasses and caps on back-to-front. After forgetting his lines, he decided to freestyle Vanilla Ice's *Ice Ice Baby* lyrics which he had learnt from Mum's novelty Christmas toy penguin. The other wise men didn't look too impressed, but the audience loved it!

My class's performance of our *Home Alone* take of the nativity went down a storm. I even managed to suppress the urge to buck Evil Emily from the donkey when she squeezed my neck too hard on purpose.

The biggest highlight for me, though, was looking out into the audience and seeing not just Mum, Dad and Little Spud watching me, but Rob, Cassie, and my baby half-sister, Jodie, too. Rob was sitting next to Dad, and Mum even had Jodie on her lap at one point.

It was great that Mum and Rob got on well enough now to sit together like that. He may not have been there for me over the years like a biological dad should, but it meant a lot to me that he had made the effort to come tonight. Maybe having Jodie had made him realise what being a dad was actually all about, and that there was more to it than turning up once a month to take me to the arcade.

The play climaxed with all of the teachers coming to centre stage and singing a medley of Christmas pop songs. They started off singing a very serious 'Oh Come All Ye Faithful,' and then shocked the whole room by whipping off their sensible black cloaks to reveal sparkly jump suits as they started belting out 'Merry Christmas Everybody' by Slade. We all stood there dumbfounded, as Mr Growler took the microphone as lead vocalist.

Who would have thought our headmaster would have such a good singing voice? Mum always told me that there was a lot more to people than met the eye, and that was obviously the case with Mr Growler!

By the time the teachers had finished their medley, the entire audience were up on their feet clapping along. Mrs Jackson, Mr Growler, Mrs Ramsbottom and all of the other teachers, who usually seemed so strict and boring, took a bow to shouts of 'Encore, encore!' which I knew meant 'again' in French.

Obviously on a high from all of the applause, Mr Growler started singing 'All I want for Christmas is You' by Mariah Carey, with the Year Five teaching assistants as his backing singers. He even managed to hit the high notes! If he ever got sacked from teaching, he could get a job as a pop star at this rate!

Mr Growler had been right. This really was the best Christmas show that

Summercroft School had ever done! If I couldn't find out the identity of the secret Father Christmas, maybe I could write my newspaper article about it. I could see it now...

"NOT SO BORING HEADTEACHER SHOCKS PUPILS AND PARENTS WITH A VOICE THAT WOULD RIVAL BRUNO MARS!"

CHAPTER 15

"So Rob has suggested that you have Christmas Eve and Christmas Day with us, and then go to him for Boxing Day," Mum said. "Is that OK with you Ben?"

We were sitting at the kitchen table drinking hot chocolate and marshmallows, and eating chocolate chip cookies. It was way past Little Spud and Big Spud's bedtime, but we were all far too excited after the Christmas show to go straight to bed. Mum said we could all stay up late as a special treat.

"Yeah, that's fine," I said. "I'd rather be here for Christmas Eve as Rob doesn't do the Christmas Eve box as well as you do Mum."

I was referring to the special box that Mum had given to each of us on Christmas Eve for as long as I could remember. It was a shoebox wrapped in Christmas paper. Inside, we would always get a new pair of pyjamas, a sachet of extra tasty hot chocolate, a small packet of mini marshmallows tied up with a gold and red striped ribbon, and a new book to read as we went to bed on Christmas Eve. It had become a tradition we all loved.

Mum and Dad giggled as they remembered my recount of Christmas Eve at Rob's last year. Knowing that I loved spending Christmas with Mum, Dad and my brothers, his competitive side had come out and he'd tried to make it even better at his house. I always felt sad leaving my brothers to see to my 'other dad' over Christmas. I didn't usually mind the fact that Dad was actually all of their real dad but mine was Rob. Dad always treated me exactly the same as all of them, and I couldn't even remember life before he came along as he and Mum met when I was still a baby. But Christmas time just wasn't the same without all of my annoying brothers around me. At least I would have my new baby sister, Jodie, there this year. That would be much better than just me, Rob and Cassie.

"What are you laughing at?" whined Pocket Rocket, hating the fact that he wasn't in on the joke.

"Rob's attempt at a Christmas Eve box," said Mum. "He completely misunderstood the whole concept, and had wrapped an empty shoe box in Christmas paper with nothing in it. He thought you were meant to leave it out for Father Christmas to fill with presents instead of a stocking!"

“Poor Ben was so disappointed when he opened it up to find an empty box,” laughed Dad. “Rob even captured the moment on camera, expecting Ben to be excited when he gave it to him. It was so funny!”

“No it wasn’t,” I said crossly. Although a year later, I was starting to see the funny side. I was definitely going to have to give Rob some tips on how to give Jodie a good Christmas. Perhaps Mum would even invite her to ours one year like one big happy family. Mum, Dad, me, Pocket Rocket, Big Spud, Little Spud, Rob, Cassie, and Jodie.

Maybe I would suggest that for next year. They all seemed to be getting on well at the Christmas show.

"It's not fair," moaned Big Spud.

"What's not fair?" asked Dad.

"I want two dads like Ben," he replied. "He gets two big presents at Christmas, and two birthday presents. I want two lots of presents!"

"Yeah," piped up Little Spud. "We want two dads as well. Mum, get us another dad!"

Dad's facial expression alternated between being perplexed, amused, and slightly offended.

Rather than following up on their request for a new dad, Pocket Rocket tried a different tactic. "Or instead of getting us an extra dad, you could just give us two presents," he suggested.

Mum looked at my three little brothers, momentarily speechless.

"Just when I thought I had heard it all,"

she said after finding her voice again. "You lot never cease to amaze me. I have considered your rather interesting proposal to get you an extra dad, and although it's tempting at times," she said, winking at my dad, "I think the one we have here is worth twenty dads."

Big Spud and Little Spud jumped onto Dad's lap to give him a big hug. Pocket Rocket, on the other hand, looked at me with jealous eyes and mumbled, "I'd rather have two presents."

Dad swatted him on the bottom with a cushion as he wandered over to turn the TV on. "Oh look, it's that secret Father Christmas do-gooder again," he said as the local news came on.

"Our local angel in disguise, or Saint Christmas as locals are calling him, strikes again," came the newsreader's voice. She spoke in the sensible, direct way newsreaders always seemed to. "Just moments ago, he was captured on camera decorating the Christmas tree at the top of the high street with Christmas chocolates."

The screen zoomed in on Father Christmas, and sure enough, there he was, hanging about fifty chocolates on the tree. They were decorated in sparkly foil with pictures of reindeer on. He was attaching them to the tree with thin strands of gold ribbon.

"How lovely is that!" exclaimed Mum. "There are going to be some excited children discovering those tomorrow morning as their parents drag them round the shops."

"Would you like to drag us round the shops tomorrow?" I asked hopefully.

"No," laughed Mum. "But I will hang one chocolate each for you on the tree while you get your pyjamas on ready for bed."

We didn't need telling twice when chocolate was involved. We raced upstairs with Obi and Lola barking at our heels, wondering what all the excitement was about.

"Mum, put two chew sticks on the tree for the dogs to find too," I shouted down the stairs.

Most mums would tell the dogs to stay away from the tree for fear of them wrecking it. Not Mum though. She loved the dogs as much as I did. I knew that a few minutes from now, our tree would be slightly heavier with four yummy chocolates, and two not so yummy dog treats!

CHAPTER 16

"Right Tommy, this is serious now," I said to my best friend as we sat in his awesome tree house the following day. "I need to submit my entry to the newspaper by Monday. That means that we have to find out who Saint Christmas is this weekend. Otherwise, I will have to go with one of my other ideas."

I think if push came to shove, I could write a pretty good article about our Christmas show, but it wouldn't compare to the headline news of revealing the identity of the mystery Father Christmas in sunglasses that everyone was talking about.

"OK, let's look at the facts we have so far," said Tommy. "We know he is in fact a 'he' as you saw the stubble under his beard on that photo."

"Yep," I agreed. "Unless he is a women with a little facial hair problem like Miss

Hairy!"

Miss Hairy was the dinner lady in charge of puddings. She had a big mole on the side of her face with three long black hairs growing out of it. No matter how hard you tried, it was impossible to look at anything other than her hairy mole whilst she was dishing a big dollop of custard into your bowl.

"True," said Tommy. "But he walks like a man, too. And he has big feet."

"How do you know he has big feet?" I asked Tommy curiously.

"Look, you can see here," he said, pointing at a picture on Instagram on his phone.

Sure enough, there was a photo of Saint Christmas delivering dog treats to the local dog home. He had been captured bending down next to a dog that looked like a cross between a Labrador and a sausage dog. His black boot was almost the entire length of the dog's body.

"Yep, definitely a man," I said, nodding my head thoughtfully.

We gazed at Tommy's phone in silence as he scrolled thought the array of photos that the public had managed to catch of the man in action.

"Look here," I said, stretching my fingers across the screen of the phone to enlarge a photo. "You can see his hairy knuckles as he's putting money in that parking meter."

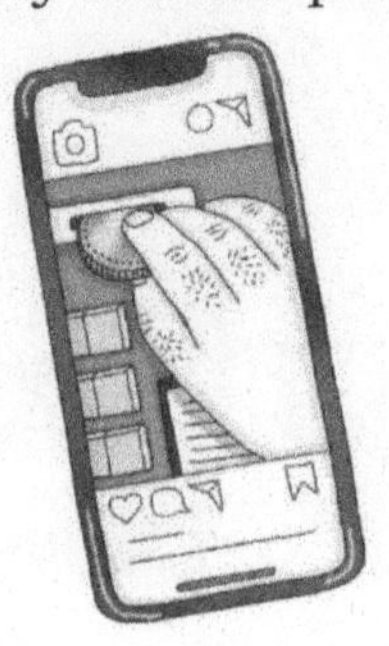

"Ew, I hope I don't get hairy knuckles when I'm older," said Tommy, screwing up his face in horror.

"Apparently it's hereditary," I told him, feeling wise. "Rob has hairy knuckles and toes! I'm just hoping I take after Mum and not him when I grow up."

"All this is doing is confirming that whoever he is, he's a man. We need something else. Like a tattoo, or the sound of his voice, or something."

"He could have a distinctive accent," I exclaimed. "That could narrow it down loads. Like if he had an Irish accent, he could be that guy who works at the café down the road from school."

"Yeah, and if he had an Australian accent, he could be that guy who you heard calling his dog Benny Boy in the park. That was so funny when you turned around to answer him, thinking he was talking to you!"

"Hilarious!" I replied sarcastically. "Who

would call their dog Ben anyway? It's obviously a person's name. Dogs should be called Obi, or Lola, or Princess... not Ben.

"Princess?" questioned Tommy dubiously.

"Well, of course I wouldn't call a dog Princess. It's just an example. Like Lottie's dog."

I hadn't spoken to my (girl)friend Lottie for two whole weeks. I made a mental note to call her sometime over Christmas. I would have to stay up really late and then sneak under my covers to call her whilst Mum and Dad were asleep because of the huge time difference between Australia and England. I quickly worked out in my head that if it were about 11pm here, it would be about 8am in Australia. Not that I think about what time it is where Lottie is much, of course. That would be a bit stalker like. Honestly I don't. Maybe just once or twice a day. OK, who am I kidding? I have an excel spreadsheet printed out and hidden under my bed with all the corresponding times on! I made it a few months back, just after she moved to Australia.

Australian Time Chart	
Time in England	Time in Australia
12am	9am
9am	6pm
6pm	3am
11pm	8am

"Lola is a person's name as well," said Tommy, determined not to let it drop.

"OK, OK," I said admitting defeat as he snapped me out of my Lottie-induced daydream. "I guess dogs can be called Ben too."

"So Benny Boy, let's see if anyone has uploaded a video of this guy so we can hear his voice," said Tommy.

"Great idea," I replied. "But I warn you now, if you call me Benny Boy again, we might have a replay of the time you fell out of the tree house courtesy of my overzealous cushion throwing. Capiche?"

"OK BEN," he said, saying my name slowly and deliberately.

I scrolled through the mass array of pictures that people had been uploading to Instagram.

"Wait, go back," said Tommy. "Look there. There's a video of him when he was doing that ridiculous dancing in the town centre to make people laugh."

Somebody had managed to get so close to Saint Christmas that they hadn't just captured his embarrassing dancing – they had also captured his atrocious singing! Not only was he busting some rather questionable dance moves to 'Uptown Funk', he was also singing along!

I sat there alongside Tommy, my mouth opening wider and wider in disbelief. Those dance moves... that singing voice. They were unmistakable! There was only one person in this town who sang as badly as that, and danced like there was no one watching – when in fact hundreds of people were watching.

"I know who it is," I said in a barely audible voice.

"What?" said Tommy, still gazing at the screen for clues.

"I know who Saint Christmas is," I said again, more loudly this time.

Tommy looked at me with wide eyes.

"Benny Bo... sorry, Ben," he said. "There are thousands of people living in and around Guildford. How on earth could you possibly know this person?"

"I promise you, I know him," I replied, with a more confident tone this time.

"Grab a notebook and pen," I said, grinning. "We are about to make front page news!"

CHAPTER 17

"Ben, I can't just drop everything to take you and Tommy into town," said Mum. "I've got your brothers to look after."

"Bring them with us!" I said, exasperated. It was times like this I had to bite my tongue to stop myself from asking Mum why she had thought it was a good idea to have so many children.

"Let's all go," said Dad walking into the room. "We can all get our Secret Santa presents while we're there."

Every year, we had a little tradition where we picked a name out of a hat and had to secretly buy that person a present for under £5. Dad had moaned that it should be called Secret Father Christmas, as Secret Santa sounded too American, but it didn't have quite the same ring to it. I did try to tell him that the word Santa actually had origins in the Dutch word Sinta Klaus, and not America, but he didn't listen. He can be pretty stubborn when he thinks he's right about something. Especially when it is something to do with being British.

"Yeah, let's go," shouted Pocket Rocket, wandering into the room. "We can see if there are any Christmas chocolates left on the Christmas tree in the town centre."

"You never know," said Dad. "Maybe Saint Christmas will be doing something in the town centre again today. We might catch him in the act. Did anyone notice that he seems to do his random acts of kindness every Wednesday and Saturday?"

Dad was right. I had thought the same thing myself whilst in detective mode. The mystery man's random acts often took place at random times, but he never failed to do something on a Saturday, and it had always been in the town centre itself, hence why I was so keen to get Mum to take me and Tommy there today. I was willing to bet money on the fact that he would be there again. This was my chance to catch him in the act, even if it meant searching around town all day.

"Come on, let's go," I shouted impatiently.

"OK," said Mum. "Shoes on everyone."

We all rushed into the hall. Me, on my mission to discover the identity of Saint Christmas. Pocket Rocket, on a mission to get to the town centre Christmas tree in the hope of finding a chocolate that others may have missed. Big Spud, eager to buy his Secret Santa present for Little Spud. He never could keep a secret, and had told me about thirty seconds after discovering who he was buying for, after almost bursting with trying to not blurt it out. Hang on a minute, where was Little Spud?

"LITTLE SPUD!" I shouted.

"Coming," came his little muffled voice from his bedroom. "I just need to find my Batman cape."

I smacked my hand to my forehead in exasperation. Why, oh why, did my little brother have to dress up every time we left the house? I could see now why Mum got so stressed when she was trying to get us all out. I now understood why she kept a spare pair of swimming goggles handy when he was going through his phase of dressing up in a fireman helmet complimented by a set of goggles.

"Your cape is still on Obi," shouted Mum, as Obi wandered into the hallway looking hopeful.

"Sorry boy, not this time," I said as I stroked his long floppy ears. "I'll take you out later, I promise."

Obi was dressed up in a Batman cape, courtesy of Little Spud coaxing him into playing superheroes earlier. He had got off lightly. Poor Lola was wearing Mum's Wonder Woman skirt and headband!

Mum tells people that she got it for a fancy dress party years ago. The truth is that she bought it to dress up in and run around the house with us when we were younger, and all used to play superheroes together. She forgot she had it on one day, and opened the door to someone whilst in the middle of a very important mission to save the world from the evil Doctor Doom. Trust me, it wasn't a good look to meet your new neighbour who was popping round to introduce themselves.

Shortly after that, Mum's Wonder Woman outfit found its way into Little Spud's dressing up box. Today, it was apparently Lola's turn to play dress up!

Fifteen tortuous minutes later, we reversed out of the driveway and headed for the town centre.

"So, why exactly are you so keen to go into town this afternoon Ben?" Mum asked me suspiciously.

"Like Dad said," I answered innocently. "I need to get my Secret Santa present."

"Are you buying it for me?" asked Little Spud excitedly. "I fink everyone should get it for me coz I'm the littlest!"

"Maybe," I said, as his lips curled up into a satisfied smile. "But then again, maybe not." I said, teasing him.

His smile quickly evaporated. "Mum, Ben's being mean to me," he whined.

"Ben, leave your brother alone," Mum said, turning round to glare at me. "Could you boys for once get in this car without winding each other up?"

Little Spud looked at me smugly and stuck his tongue out, satisfied that I had received the 'Mum look of disapproval.'

Suddenly, I didn't feel so guilty about Pocket Rocket tricking him and Big Spud into doing all of our chores throughout December. Little brothers were so annoying sometimes.

"If you are my Secret Santa, I'm going to buy you a second hand pair of smelly socks," I whispered loudly to Little Spud, feeling childish.

"Shh," snapped Dad, as he turned up the radio. "Listen!"

The DJ on the local radio station was talking very excitedly. I listened as I caught the sentence midway through.

"...he'll only come down when crowds have donated at least £10,000 to little five-year-old Darcey Edwards, who needs to go to America for some ground breaking treatment to save her life."

Everyone knew about Darcey. She had a rare disease that could only be treated in America, and her parents couldn't afford the treatment. They had been doing all kinds of fundraising events but still didn't have enough.

"Come on folks. Get yourself down to Guildford Cathedral now to see the man in action. Forget the Father Christmas from Lapland. We have our very own Father Christmas in Guildford who is an absolute saint," the DJ went on.

I couldn't believe my luck. After hoping that by some slim chance of luck, I might spot the man himself doing a little act of kindness on the streets of Guildford, I was now going to witness him first hand doing something massive. All of his little acts of kindness must have been leading up to this one ultimate finale. And I was going to be there to record every second of it, before unveiling his true identity to the public.

CHAPTER 18

Dad didn't take much convincing to take a right at the next roundabout instead of turning left to the town centre car parks. I think the whole family were excited to see what Saint Christmas was up to now.

"Do you think he's climbed up a tree next to the cathedral?" asked Big Spud.

"I bet he's climbed up the flag pole," joined in Pocket Rocket.

"We'll soon find out," said Mum, as we pulled into the car park. We saw groups of people walking in the direction of the cathedral as Dad pulled up the car's handbrake. Apparently, we weren't the only ones who had been listening to the radio. We all clambered out of the car, and raced towards the cathedral to see what was going on. We stopped and looked up in shock as we arrived at where a crowd was quickly gathering. All eyes were gazing upwards. Saint Christmas wasn't up a tree.

He wasn't even up the flag pole. There, 160 foot off the ground, sitting next to the angel statue, was the unmistakeable Father Christmas costume, fake beard, and sunglasses. He was sitting like he didn't have a care in the world at the top of the cathedral itself!

I looked up feeling a little anxious. What if he slipped and fell? Mum followed my gaze and read my mind.

"Look," she said pointing up. "He's got a rope tied around his waist. He must be planning on abseiling down when he's raised enough money for little Darcey."

I gazed around me at the ever growing crowd. There must have been about 200 people there, and others were still walking up from the car park. There was a sudden crackling sound as Saint Christmas raised a megaphone to his lips. I hadn't even noticed it sitting next to him. He was so far up, it looked the size of the jug from Little Spud's toy tea party set (please don't ask me why my little brother has such a girly toy. Let's just say Mum is to blame for that one!)

"HO HO HO," came a crackly voice through the crowds. He was so high up that the sound travelled effortlessly above us in the wind.

The crowd cheered at the sound of his voice. Mum and Dad grinned at us. This was turning into quite a day out. Everyone was really getting into the spirit of things.

"If you raise £10,000 for little Darcey, I will abseil down the cathedral," he boomed. "However, if you manage to raise £20,000, I will also reveal my true identity when I get to the bottom!"

A big cheer went up from the crowd as my face fell. This couldn't be happening. This was my story! I was going to be the one to do the big identity reveal in the article that would blow all other contestants efforts out of the water! Now Saint Christmas was going to completely ruin it.

I reached into my pocket and pulled out my mobile phone. I found the contact I was after, and started typing a text message.

`"I know it's u! Please don't tell everyone who u are. Want to write about` it 4 newspaper comp!"

I held my breath, hoping that Saint Christmas would have his mobile phone up there with him. Seconds later, I saw him reaching into his pocket for what must have been his phone. He was too far away for me to know for sure, but my suspicions were confirmed when I heard my own phone beep moments later.

"How did u find out? Sorry, I have 2. Could save little girl's life."

I shrugged my shoulders in defeat. He was right. What was more important? Me winning the newspaper competition? Or a little girl getting life-saving treatment? It was a no brainer.

"Ok," I text back. "U r right."

My phone pinged again, almost instantly.

“U can get exclusive interview though! That should make front page news!”

A huge grin spread across my face as I realised how huge this was. A full time, paid reporter, with twenty years’ experience would kill to get a scoop like this. And the glory was going to be all mine!

“Who are you texting?” asked Tommy.

“Oh, just Lottie,” I lied. “She wanted to speak to me, but I told her I was busy.”

I crossed my fingers behind my back so that the lie didn’t count. It was only a little porky pie anyway.

"Isn't it the middle of the night in Australia," questioned Tommy as he narrowed his eyes suspiciously at me.

"I've got a great idea," said Dad, saving me from further interrogation. "How about we all donate our Secret Santa money to this good cause. If we all put £5 in, that's £30 we can put towards helping Little Darcey."

"£30 isn't much," said Pocket Rocket. "She needs about £100,000 for that treatment, Dad."

"I know," he replied. "But just imagine. If everyone who was here now gave £5 that would be about £1000, just like that. There must be at least 200 people here already. And judging by the number of people taking photos on their phones, that number is going to double in the next half an hour. Then there's everyone else who can't come down here, but will donate anyway because it's such a good cause."

"Dad's right," said Mum. "I wonder if

Saint Christmas is actually Darcey's dad, and this was his plan all along to raise money for her treatment. I reckon they'll raise far more than the £20,000 he's asked for."

I smiled smugly to myself, knowing that I was the only person in the entire crowd who had already worked out the identity of Saint Christmas, whilst everyone else was still guessing.

"So, what do we reckon?" asked Dad. "Are you all up for it?"

Big Spud and Little Spud looked at me to see how I, as the big brother, would react. Pocket Rocket beat me to it though, surprising us all.

"Ok, I'll donate my £5," he said. I smiled at my younger brother who was usually the first to feel hard done by if his Secret Santa present was even one pence below the maximum budget of £5. Maybe my little brother was learning the art of giving and not just getting after all.

"Me too," I said.

"Me three," said Big Spud.

"Me six," said Little Spud, not quite getting the logic behind what Big Spud was saying.

"Aw, I knew you boys were listening when I kept telling you to be kind all these years," said Mum, grabbing us all into a group hug.

"I'll give £100 too Mr C," said Tommy, pulling a big wad of notes out of his pocket. He looked sheepish as my brothers looked at him with their mouths wide open.

"Dad gave it to me to buy myself a Christmas present," he said. "I'd much rather help Darcey with it. There's nothing I need anyway."

Poor Tommy. He would much rather his parents had given him something cheap and little if it meant they put a bit of thought into it. I made a mental note to ask Mum if Tommy could do Secret Santa with us next year.

"That's really kind Tommy, thanks," said Dad, taking the money. "Now, how do we go about giving the money to this crazy dare devil Saint Christmas.

Right on cue, Saint Christmas held up his megaphone to make an announcement.

"Ho Ho Ho, if any of you lovely lot would like to donate to this great cause, there is a JustGiving page you can connect to right now on your mobile phones. It's titled Do it for Darcey! Come on everyone. Do it now and I'll put you on my nice list!"

I looked around me and saw a sea of

hands holding mobile phones. Every onlooker seemed to be in a trance, doing exactly what Saint Christmas had told them to do. He would raise enough money to help Darcey ten times over at this rate. What an amazing thing to witness. Dad put the cash in his pocket, and pulled out his phone to do the same. "I'll transfer £130 from my bank account now," he said.

"Does that mean you can use the cash to buy us all something yummy?" asked Pocket Rocket, never one to miss an opportunity.

He caught Dad at the right time though, on a high from all the feel-good vibes around us. He responded with, "Sure, why not. Let's use it for a take-away pizza tonight," which was met with nods of approval from all of us. You couldn't beat a good pepperoni pizza night. Maybe now was a good time to ask Dad to grab us a few tubs of cookie dough ice cream for pudding!

"This is crazy!" said Dad, looking at his

phone in astonishment. “Look at this, boys!”

We all crowded round his phone, and watched as the total on the ‘Do-it-for-Darcey’ page rose second by second. It quickly changed from £150 to £1000 to £2000 to £3000...

“Wow, that’s a lot of money!” I exclaimed.

“There are a lot of people with good hearts out there,” said Mum.

I glanced up at Saint Christmas, feeling nothing but admiration and pride. All around me, people were standing, almost in silence, looking at their phones. They were undoubtedly doing exactly the same as we were, and watching the total raise by the second. I quickly looked back down at Dad’s phone as I heard someone shout, “It’s hit £10,000!” It didn’t stop there, though. The amount just kept going up and up and up. It was only a matter of time before Saint Christmas was going to abseil down the cathedral and reveal his true identity to the waiting masses, and I wanted a front row seat!

CHAPTER 19

"Wow, you guys are amazing!" boomed a voice down the megaphone fifteen minutes later. It was Saint Christmas.

The target of £20,000 on the 'Do-it-for-Darcey' page had been surpassed just moments before and was still increasing.

"I had planned on spending the night up here," joked Saint Christmas. "But thanks to you giving bunch, I will abseil down this impressive cathedral any moment now and reveal my identity to you."

A massive cheer of excitement went up from the crowd. They were finally going to find out who this amazing man was, who had done so many acts of kindness this past month.

I looked up to the top of the cathedral, feeling both anxious and excited all at once. It was like the feeling you get when you're queueing up to go on a really fast roller coaster. You want the thrill of it, but at the same time your stomach feels like it's got hundreds of butterflies flapping around in it because you're so nervous.

A countdown started amongst the crowd, as Saint Christmas stood up and leaned backwards, ready to make his descent down the cathedral wall. I felt my nails digging into the palms of my hands where they were clenched with nerves.

"I hope his rope is tight enough," said Mum, looking slightly anxious herself.

"Imagine if he ended up going splat!" said Big Spud.

"That would be funny," giggled Little Spud.

“Oi, shut up you two,” I said frowning at them. “This isn’t one of the stupid TV shows you watch. This is real life. He’s a real person, you know!”

This, along with Mum’s look of disapproval, stopped their childish giggles straight away. Their little faces gazed up at the cathedral with a new seriousness to them.

“Look, he’s half-way down,” shouted Pocket Rocket, pointing upwards.

Sure enough, Saint Christmas had already expertly abseiled down half of the 160-foot-tall building. He went out of sight momentarily and my heart skipped a beat.

"Where's he gone?" I muttered to no one in particular.

"He needs to walk along that bit of the roof there to abseil down the last part of the wall," explained Dad matter-of-factly, like people did this kind of thing every day,

"Look, he's there!" shouted Tommy.

Saint Christmas was making his way down the last part of the cathedral wall. Any minute now he would be on the ground and the crowd would swarm around him, eager to get the first photos of the man himself.

"Come on," I said, grabbing Big Spud and Little Spud's hands. "We need to get over there." Knowing that Mum and Dad would have no choice but to follow the trail of my younger brothers, I weaved them in and out of the crowds to get as close to the edge of the cathedral as possible. I had been watching the whole thing unravel so intently that I didn't notice how many hundreds of people had arrived to watch this dare-devil fundraiser. Lines of people were now stretching across the entire perimeter of the cathedral. There must have been about a thousand people there. I once again felt a surge of pride, knowing that the identity of the mystery man was about to be revealed. The man who by now must have raised well over the £100,000 that little Darcey's family needed for her treatment. And I knew him!

My little brothers were practically flying next to me, their little feet barely skimming the ground as I sped them along.

We reached the right side of the cathedral just as Saint Christmas was descending the last few metres of the wall. Mum, Dad, Pocket Rocket, and Tommy arrived seconds behind us.

"Ben, you shouldn't have charged off with your little brothers like that," reprimanded Mum in between puffs. Oh good, she was too worn out from running to give a long lecture! Before she could catch her breath again, I ran over to Saint Christmas and flung my arms around him just as his feet touched the ground.

He removed his sunglasses to reveal his eyes, and I immediately knew that my suspicions were right. Thank goodness – it would have been rather embarrassing if this had actually turned out to be a stranger I was hugging. That would be a real cringe moment!

I glanced over at Mum, Dad, and my brothers, and saw them looking confused at my uncharacteristic behaviour. Only Tommy had a knowing smile on his face where he had obviously put two and two together, and worked out what I was up to.

Saint Christmas then picked up the megaphone that he had tied around his waist whilst he was abseiling down.

"Ladies and Gentleman, boys and girls. Thank you so much for your amazingly generous donations for little Darcey. Thanks to all of you, we now have double what she needed for her treatment, which means that we can donate the rest to other sick children too!"

A huge cheer went up from the cathedral grounds. You could almost feel the happiness oozing out of everyone.

"Now, as promised," he said dramatically, "I will reveal my true identity to you."

I grinned over at Mum as Saint Christmas whipped off his hat and fake beard to a massive round of applause. I saw her mouth drop open so wide her chin almost hit the ground. "I knew I recognised that voice!" she said in shock.

CHAPTER 20

1 Week Later – Christmas Eve

"Come on Mum, hurry up," I yelled impatiently.

"I'll be down in a minute," Mum replied. "Just as soon as I've found Little Spud."

I groaned and rubbed my left eyebrow in frustration. Once again, my little brother was making it difficult to leave the house.

"Found him!" shouted Pocket Rocket laughing.

I raced up the stairs to see what was so funny, momentarily forgetting my haste to go out. I followed Mum into Little Spud's bedroom. Little Spud was lying in his bed, dressed in the pyjamas that he had received in his Christmas Eve box last year. He was cuddling his favourite soft toy dog, and doing a very unconvincing fake snore.

"Hguuu shoooo hguuu shoooo," went his little voice. He made his lips into a big, over the top circle as he puffed out the 'shoooo' sound.

"What on earth are you doing?" exclaimed Mum. "Those pyjamas don't even fit you anymore. And more to the point, I helped you get dressed an hour ago!"

Little Spud ignored her and carried on snoring.

"Oi," I said as I reached out to tickle his feet. "We know you're not asleep."

One of Little Spud's eyes popped open as he scrunched his ticklish feet up to his body in attempt to avoid my hand.

"I'm tricking Father Christmas into coming early," he whispered.

"That's a good idea," said Big Spud excitedly as he ran into the room. He clambered past the rest of us and jumped under the covers next to Little Spud. Following his younger brother's lead, he too closed his eyes and started fake-snoring.

"Nice try, boys," said Mum. "But Father Christmas isn't silly. He won't be stepping foot in this house until the stars are glistening, and there's a mince pie and a nice glass of milk at the bottom of the fireplace."

"I thought he liked beer, not milk," piped up Pocket Rocket. "That's what Dad always says."

Mum ignored him, and pulled the duvet from my two little brothers.

"Come on, you two. You're just going to have to go to bed tonight like all the other children in the world and hope that Father Christmas pays you a visit whilst you really are fast asleep, dreaming of reindeer and elves."

Big Spud and Little Spud sat up, looking very annoyed that Mum had spoilt their plan.

"OK," said Big Spud, "but we're going to bed really early tonight and you can't stop us!"

Mum laughed. "You won't have any arguments from me there," she said.

"Can we go now Mum?" I asked with an agitated tone.

"Calm down Ben, it's 10am. I don't think the shop will have sold out of newspapers already."

It was Christmas Eve. The day that the winner of the newspaper competition would be revealed. The winning article was actually being printed on the front page of today's newspaper, and no one knew who the winner was yet. If you hadn't already guessed, I was more than a little excited.

"You know Ben, you mustn't be disappointed if you haven't won," said Mum in a gentle voice. "There were hundreds of entries and there can only be one winner. Hopefully it is you, but if it's not, you should feel very proud of what you wrote anyway."

"Yes, yes Mum, I know, it's not all about the winning but the taking part, blahdy, blahdy, blah," I said irritably.

With all of my brothers finally out of the house, we all jumped into the car and drove to the shop round the corner. Little Spud was still in his pyjamas after refusing to take them off. Mum had bundled an old

Acknowledgements

Thank you to all those who helped with this project, especially Dewi Eburne for his huge encouragement, Rich Bicknell for his ongoing pestering to get it into print, John Deacon for his helpful suggestions regarding the prologue and to Alice Bicknell for her excellent map design. Thanks also to my son Caleb and daughter Stacey for reading the drafts so quickly and pointing out various errors that needed correcting. Thank you to my youngest son Josiah's positive feedback, and to my wife for her encouragements, direction and suggestions. Finally, my deepest thanks go to my Creator who supplied the time, energy, ideas and the people around me, thus making the whole project possible. To the Lord, whose real world is far more sophisticated than any imaginary world I could invent, and whose final kingdom is far more wonderful than any fantasy world ever could be – to Him be all glory.

Read More Ref Light